odd tales...

The material printed in this collection originally appeared in
Devilboy in the Land of Love- 1996, The Boy Who ate the World-1997,
The Old Woman in the Shoe-1998, The Snow Prince-2001, The Stopping of Harold-2006 and The Angry Drunk
Graphics Holiday Spectacular #5 2010. All contents © 2011 Steve Vincent. Permission to quote or reproduce material
for reviews or notices must be obtained from the publisher (info@AngryDrunkGraphics.com).

Published by Angry Drunk Graphics / Burke   isbn 978-0-9856317-0-3   Printed in the U.S.A.

MELISSA

There once was a girl named Melissa,
who could only inhale through
her toes.

She used to make fun of her best
friend Jill,
since she had to inhale through
her nose.

Then one rainy day,
in the middle of May,
as the rain came pouring down...

Little Melissa, while making fun of
her friend,
stepped in a puddle and drowned.

DEATH LEARNED AT AN EARLY AGE, THERE WERE CERTAIN GAMES HE JUST COULDN'T PLAY

SISTERS

A long time ago on a cold Arctic shore. There once lived two sisters, Marlene and Lenore.

They were always real jealous of what each other had.

And they'd flaunt all their stuff to make each other mad.

They fought over everything that they could see.

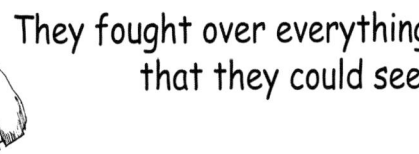

They lived their whole lives filled with envy and greed.

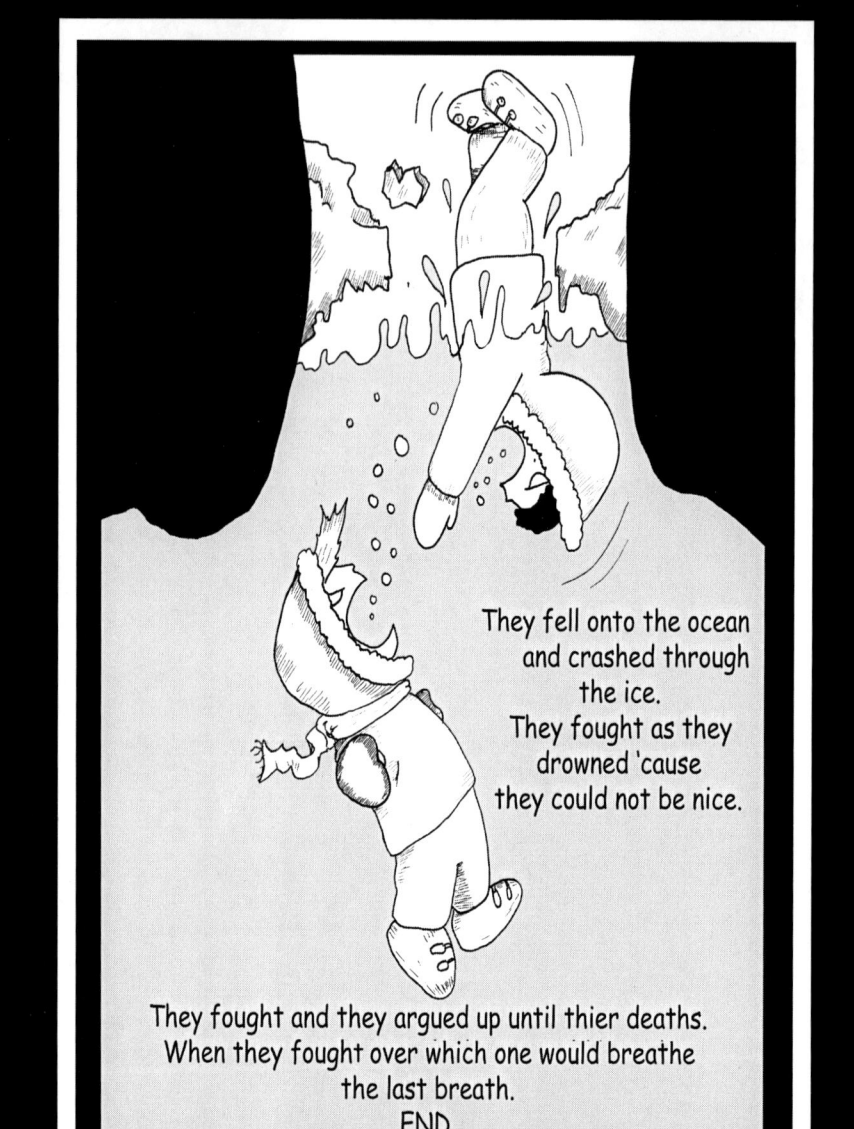

Night

There's a strange little boy who comes out at night
He likes to do things that I know are not right.

He'll hide all my socks, and he writes on the walls.
He takes my mom's dishes and then breaks them all.

He opens the windows and lets in the cold air.
He sneaks in my dad's room and cuts all his hair.

He shaved the dog once and dumps dirt on the rugs.
He fills up the cupboards with lizards and bugs.

One time he painted the TV screen red.
And he loves to put thumbtacks in my parents' bed.

He hides from my parents so they just can't see
And when they wake up, they blame it on me.

They make me eat pills and the boy goes away
But I know he'll come back even stronger someday

Just last September, a new kid moved
to town.
His head was enormous and curiously round.

When he came to school all the kids stared.
But he didn't notice
or seem to care.

He just sat at his desk and stared at the wall.
He never said anything, nothing at all.

The kids would all tease him and call him rude names.
They'd say he was stupid, or maybe insane.

The new kid just took it, never fought back at all.
He just sat there and smiled, and stared at the wall.

Then one day he smiled a big monstrous grin...

he opened his mouth

and he put Bobby in

He chewed him up slowly and with a "gulp" he was gone.

One minute later he ate Kim and Ron.

He ate Mike and Steve and Timmy and Sue

He ate all their books

and he ate their desks too.

We did all our school work,
had recess and lunch.

Then the whole town was swallowed
with one big, loud "CRUNCH"

But he didn't stop there,
he just ate and ate

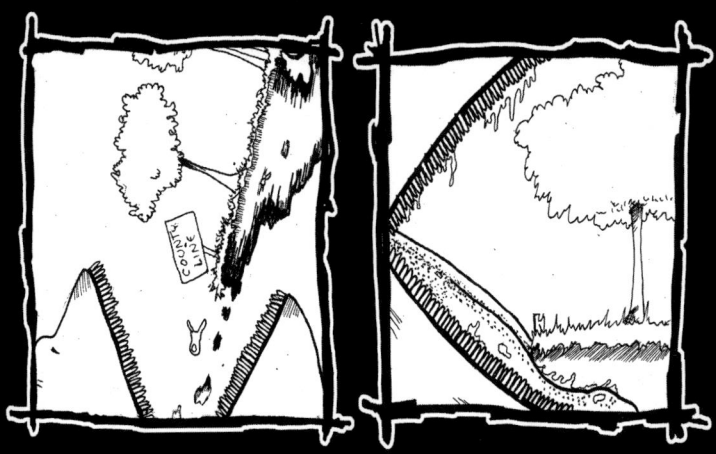

not just our town, but the county,
the state

He ate all the cities,
he ate all the plains

He ate the whole east coast
from Georgia to Maine

We hoped he would stop
but he ate the whole world.

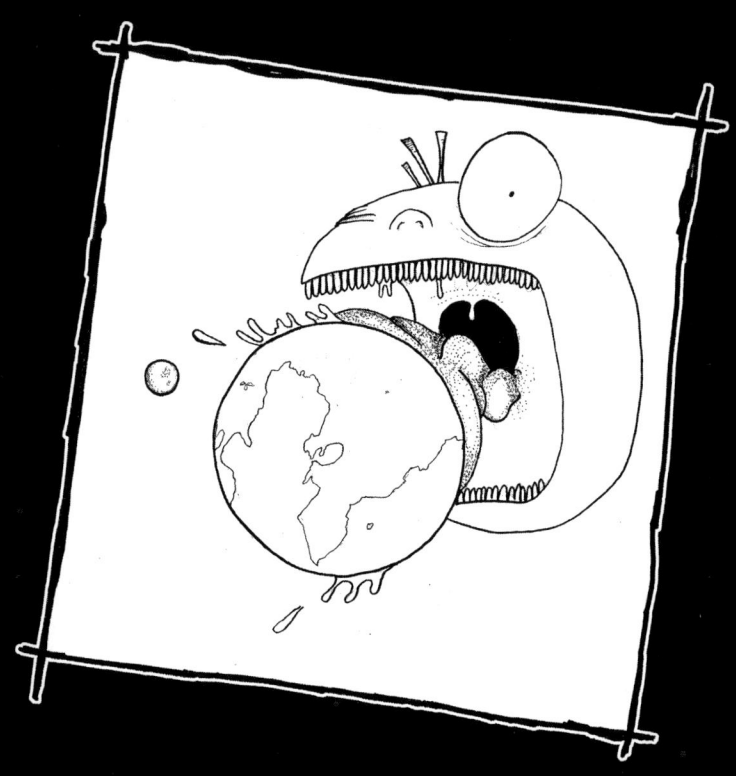

He ate all the grown ups,
the boys and the girls.

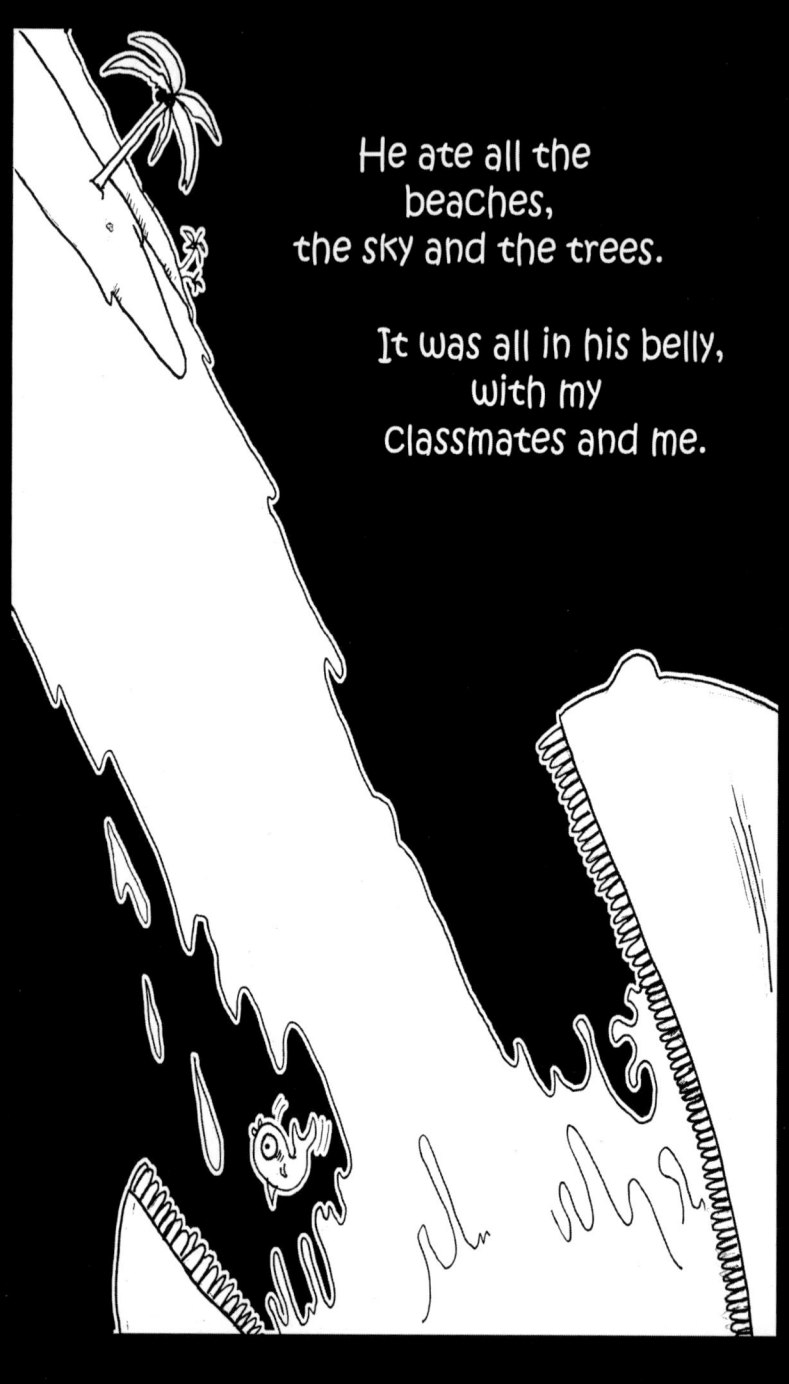

Not much has changed
in fact you can't really tell

It's just a bit warmer
and there's an odd little smell.

Actually no one believes they were eaten alive.
When I told my parents they said "don't tell lies."

And if you don't believe me I really don't care,
I know I was swallowed by that new kid who stared.

And whenever a new star or planet is found,
I know it's the new kid just gulping it down.

THE END

A Forbidden Love

A boy made out of fire,
and a girl made out of ice

Once felt a forbidden love
and paid a heavy price

On the day they finally kissed,
it was everything they feared.

As soon as they embraced each other,
they both disappeared.

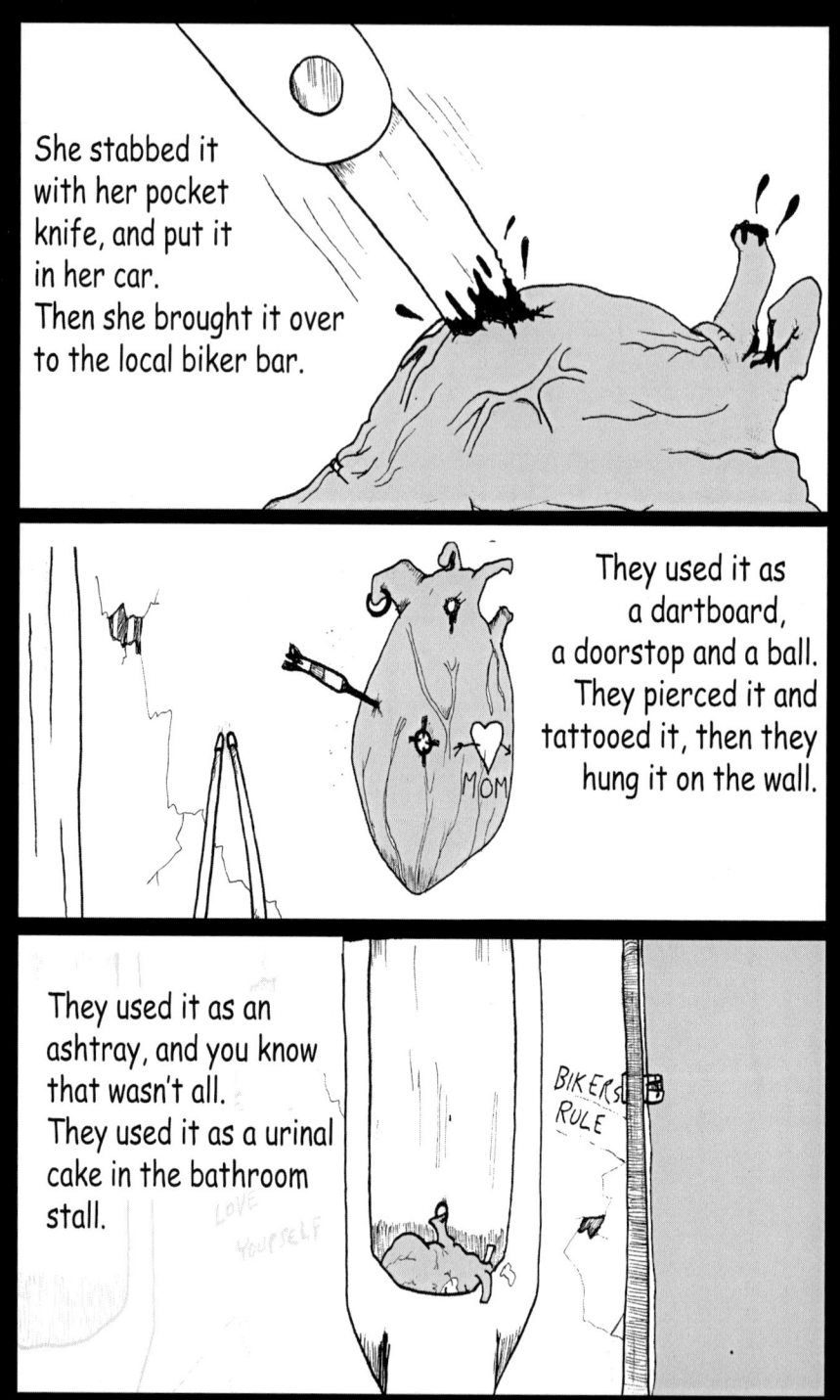

**WACK
WACK
WACK
WACK
WACK**

When she was done she picked it up
and slammed it in the door.
Then she beat it with a baseball bat
a thousand times or more.

She gave it to a homeless man
who cooked it in a stew.
By the time she gave it back to me
it was just some lumpy goo.

I sadly stuck it in my chest
and though i felt quite bad.
I think it was the best
break up
that I've ever had.

end.

Security

Poor, Poor Miss Lautenburg, look what you have done.
With all of your worrying, you've smothered your poor son.

You kept him in a bubble and away from harmful smoke.
Then you pre-chewed all his food to make sure he wouldn't choke.

You made him wear a bike helmet to protect his head from harm.
Then you tied protective pads onto his legs and arms.

And don't forget the sunscreen that you smeared onto his face,
before wrapping him in bandages just to be extra safe.

You took your old throw pillows and tied them to his chest.
Covering up his armor plated, police issue vest.

You never let him go outside to run or to play.
Still you tape his pant legs closed to keep the ticks away.

You've protected him completely to show how much you care.
But you forgot to make an opening to let him have some air.

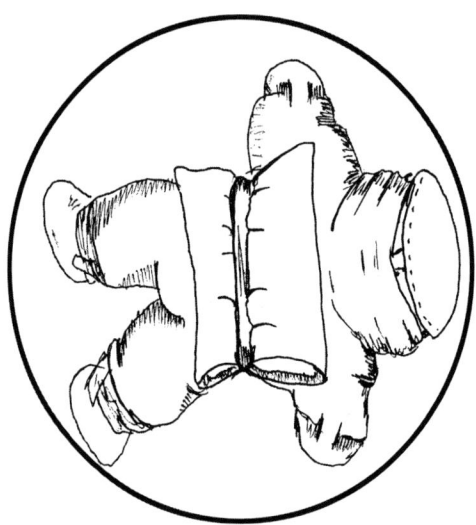

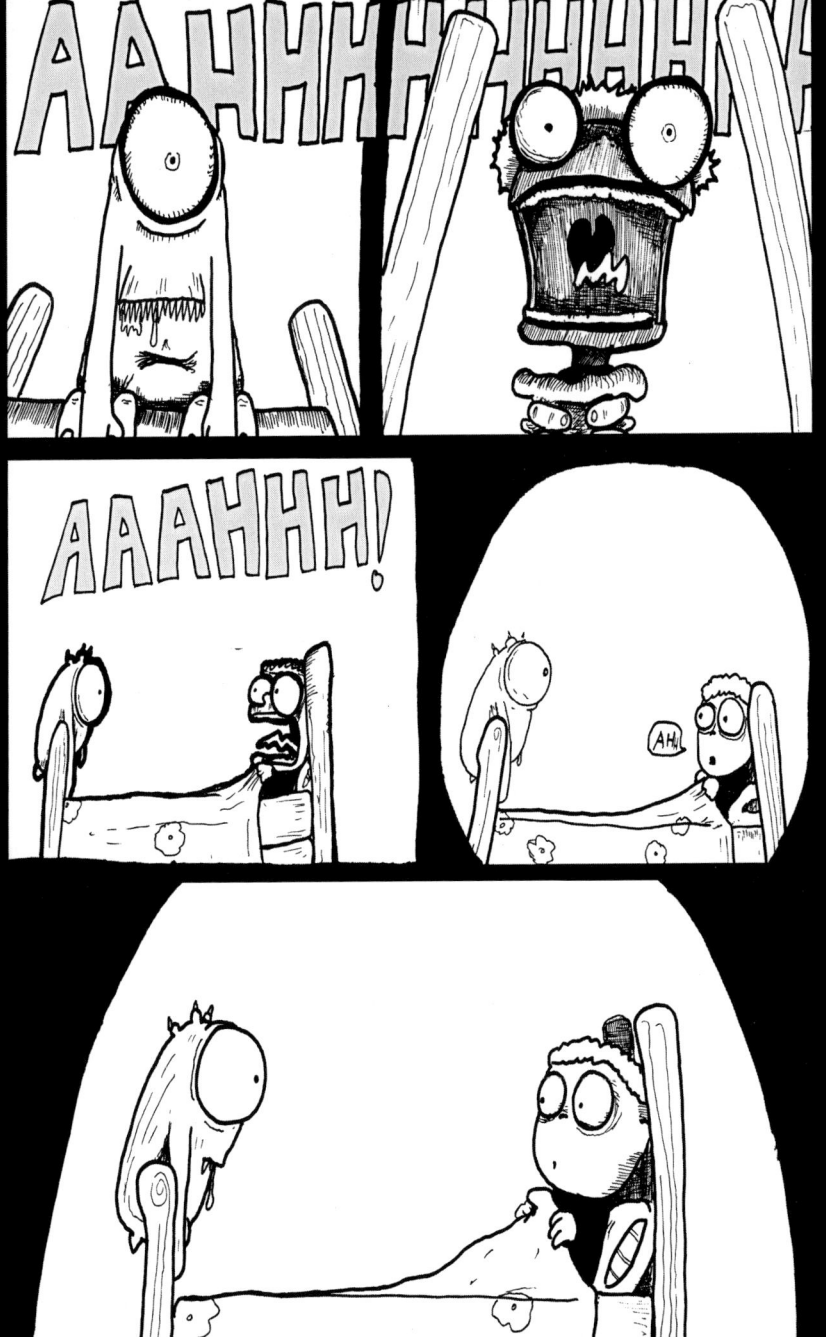

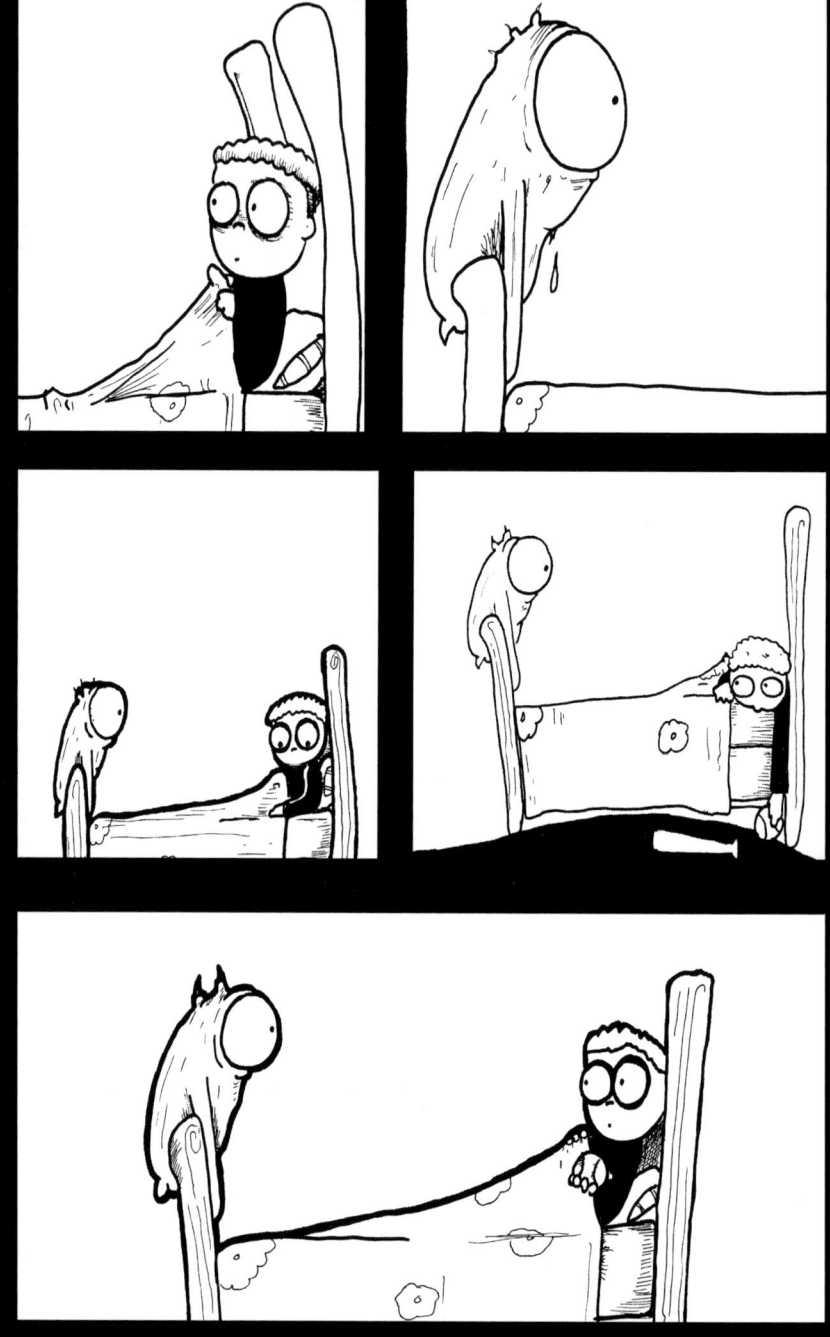

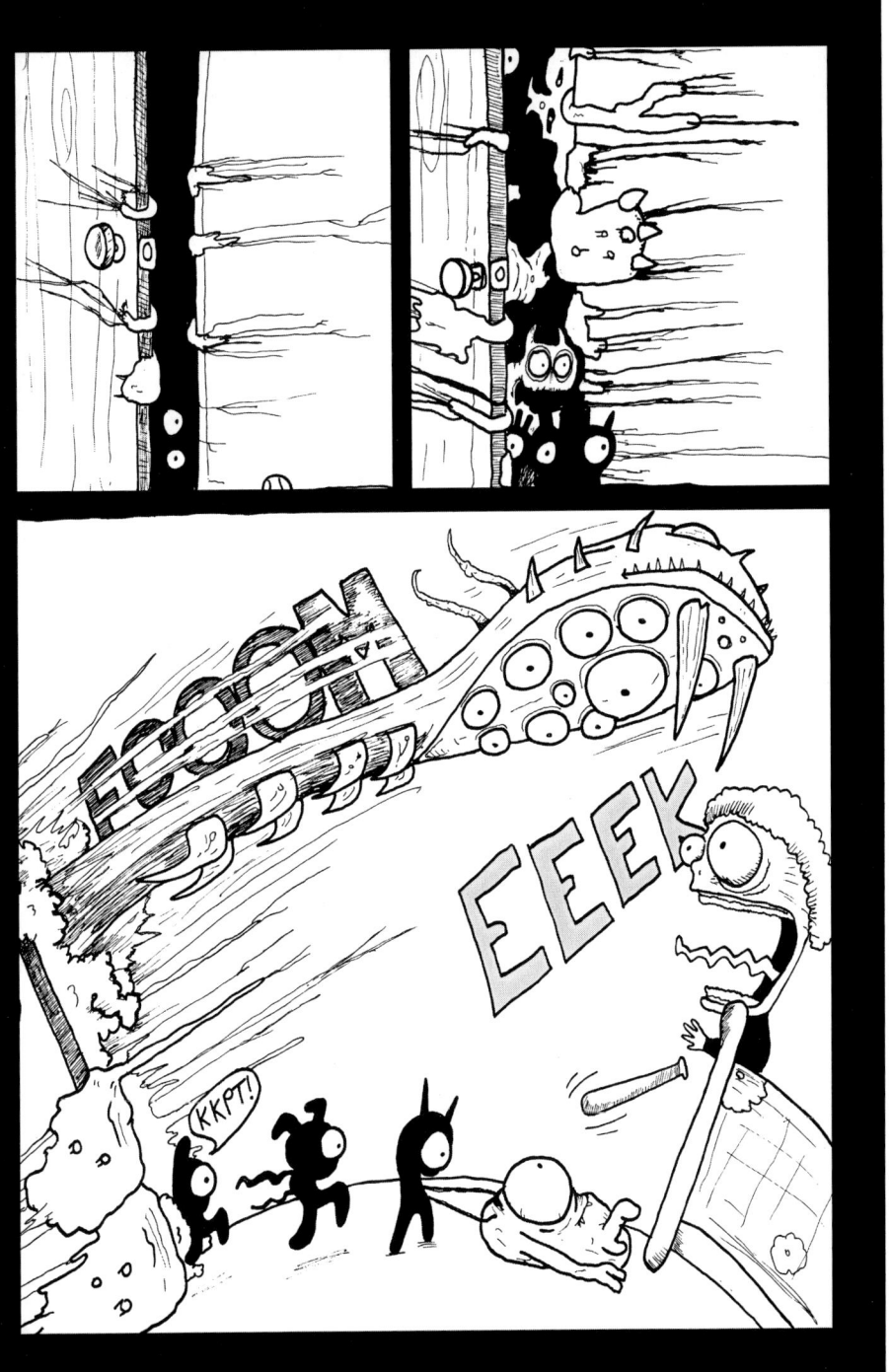

THE SNOW PRINCE

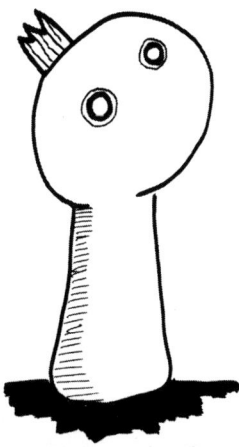

The Snow Prince

Not too long ago
in the frozen arctic tundra,
there lived a royal family of snowmen.
Five Snow Princes and a Snow King.

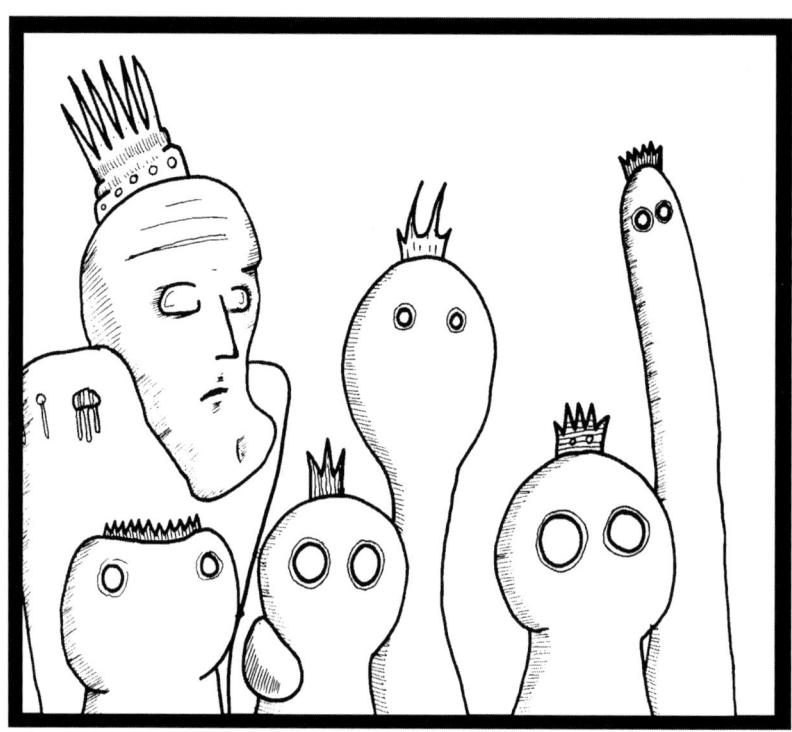

And every year when the new year arrived
a Snow Fairy would come
down from the sky
to grant a wish to one of the Princes.

Peter, the youngest Snow Prince got to make his wish last year. This year it was his older brother John's turn. But last year Peter made a stupid wish and he wanted to wish a better wish this year.

LAST YEAR...

At last! my very own Sea Monkeys!

He wanted to become a real boy.

He went to ask his dad
if he could wish his wish instead
of John. Because all
John ever wished for was cabbage
and Peter's wish
was so much better than that.

"No!" said the Snow King," You know
the rules, you have four brothers
and each of you gets a turn.
You will have your
turn in five years."

Peter didn't like that answer,
his dad had no idea
how cool his wish was,
and John still had the cabbage he
wished for five years ago.
He didn't even need any more cabbage.

That was when it dawned on him.

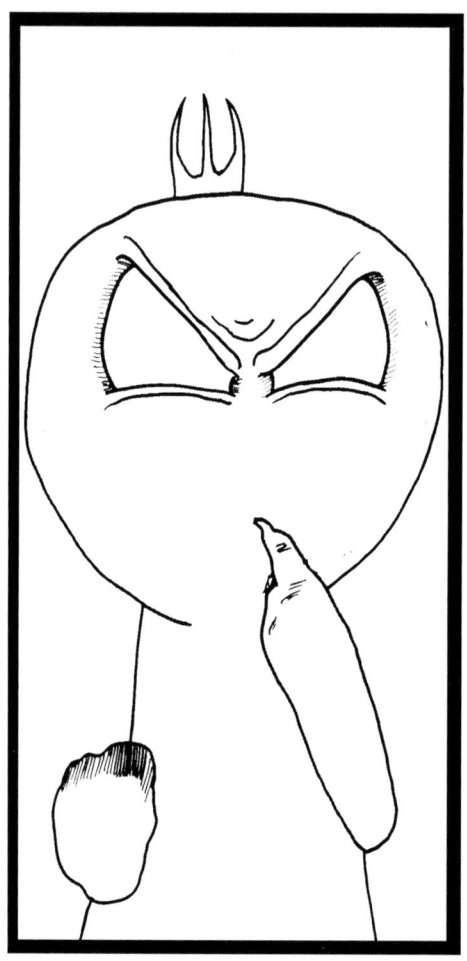

If he killed his brothers
he would get to wish his wish this year.
Not only that, he would get to wish
his wish every year !

That night he snuck into the bathroom
where his oldest brother Marcus
was getting ready for
his nightly ice bath.

When Marcus looked away Peter
poured a bag of salt into the tub.

Marcus melted in seconds.
Only three more to go thought Peter

Leaving the bathroom, he saw his second oldest brother Tim in the hall.
"Hey Tim" said Peter
"Can you do me a favor?"
"Sure, what do you need ?" asked Tim.
Tim was always ready
to do favors for people
he was the nicest of the brothers.
"I need you to hold this heated rock for me."

"Okay". said Tim taking the rock. "Whatever I can do to help".

Tim also melted in seconds. "Only two more to go" thought Peter.

"Oh my God !"
yelled Peter's other Brother Patrick.
"What happened to Tim?
He just disappeared !"
"Uh oh" thought Peter,
he didn't know Patrick was
behind him in the hall.

"He turned into that heated rock." said Peter, proud of his quick thinking. "You had better take him to dad so he can fix him." said Peter even prouder.

Patrick picked up the still warm rock and ran to show his dad.

Patrick melted before he got there.

"only one more" thought Peter.

The next morning as soon as he awoke (he decided to rest after killing three of his brothers in one night) he went into his brother John's room.

John was clearing space on his shelf for his new New Year's cabbage.

"Wanna see something cool?"
asked Peter.
"Sure I do." Said John.
"Well then take this."
said Peter handing him
a magnifying glass.
"And look at the sun,
it's beautiful this early in the morning."

"It kinda hurts" said John, right before he melted.

"Finally" thought Peter. The wishes are all mine. And not a moment too soon, that night was New Years eve. He was so excited he was shaking. Tonight he would be a real boy.

It seemed like it took forever
for night to come.
He was waiting in the wishing room
when his dad came in
"Where are your brothers Peter?"
asked the Snow King.
"I don't think they're coming"
said Peter looking down.
"They said they all had
better things to do" He lied.

"That's strange"
said the king after
waiting a couple of hours.
"John was really looking forward
to getting a new head of cabbage."
"I guess you can have his wish after all."

The king rang the bell
to call on the snow fairy.

The snow fairy arrived within minutes.

"Who gets the wish this year?"
It asked.

"I DO !" Shouted Peter.
"I WANT TO BE A REAL BOY !"

"Very well" said the Snow Fairy.
And with a wave of
his snow fairy wand he
turned Peter the Snow prince
into Peter
the real boy.

Peter looked down at his hands.
"It worked." He thought.
"I can feel the cold !" he said excitedly.

"I can feel the cold".
He repeated nervously.

Peter was frozen in seconds.

the end.

SHE WOULD MAKE THEM **FART.**

SHE'S EMBARRASSED → = FART

SHE WOULD MAKE THEM **FART ALOT.**

Poot! FART! FART STINK FART! FART! STINK! FART! Poot! FART! FART!

SO, NOBODY REALLY PICKED ON HER EVER AGAIN. AND THAT MADE HER **HAPPY.**

YAY

THE END

The edge of the World

At the edge of the world
where nobody goes.
Lives a very old man
who nobody knows.

And at the end of each day
he renames all his toes.
He might name them
Stanley or
Lester or Rose.

As soon as he's done
he takes off his
clothes.
And sticks both his feet
up into his nose.

Zombie Girl was thirteen years old
the day she came to town.
She'd been dead since she was born,
her skin was greenish brown.

Our school board didn't want her here,
in fact they tried to fight it.
But when her lawyers made a stink,
the dead girl was invited.

None of the kids would talk with her and she'd never want to play.
She just walked around real slow, moaning every day.

At recess time she'd stand real still staring at the sky.
And you couldn't eat your lunch by her because of all the flies.

She smelled real bad, she made weird sounds, she had spiders in her hair.
And to tell the truth if she disappeared no one would have cared.

One day in class her hand broke off and fell out of her sleeve.
The rotting smell got so strong, the whole school had to leave.

When we came back the boy next to me broke off both her legs.
And the whole school got sent home again for another day.

Soon every day some other kid would break another piece.
And we'd get sent home again, with a nice mid day release.

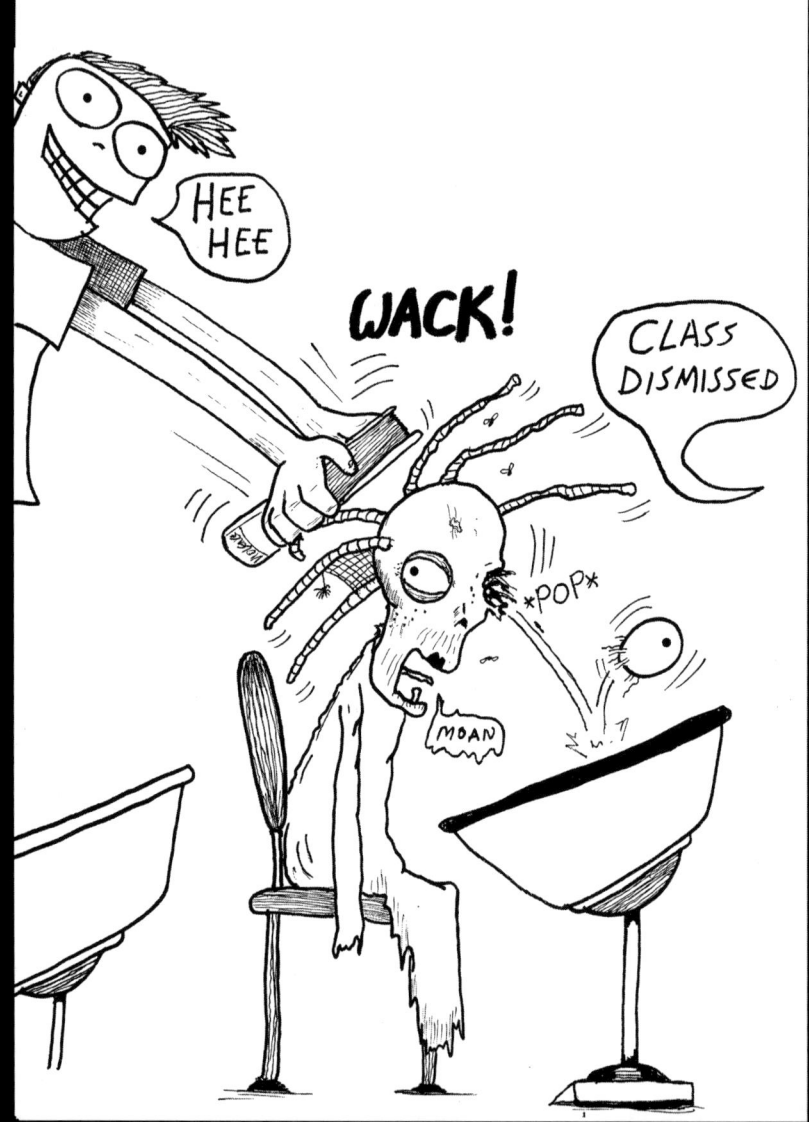

This went on for about a week,
until there was no more left to break.

Then we took what was left of her
and threw it in the lake.

It might be sad, it might be sick,
but atleast we all went home.

And please don't bother looking
for a moral to this poem.

end

THE MUNDLE-DE-GIRD

the Mundle-de-gird
shouted some words
that nobody heard
except for some birds
who thought them absurd
and then they all flew away

He yelled at the trees
who weren't very pleased
they shook all their leaves
and blew a strong breeze
He fell to his knees
and was blown out to the bay

He sat on a beach
and started to preach
when he noticed a leech
He let out a screech
and at speeds I can't reach
He turned tail and then ran away

So if you hear someone talking
an odd duck like squawking
don't stand there gawking
just keep on walking
He'll be preaching and stalking
you til the end of your days

THE BRAGGART

The Wooden Boy

There once was a boy made of wood,
who ignored all his chores.

He'd say his chores were stupid
and to do them was a bore.

He wouldn't feed his
mother's plants,
and they slowly sadly died.

And because he wouldn't
clean his room,
The junk had piled high.

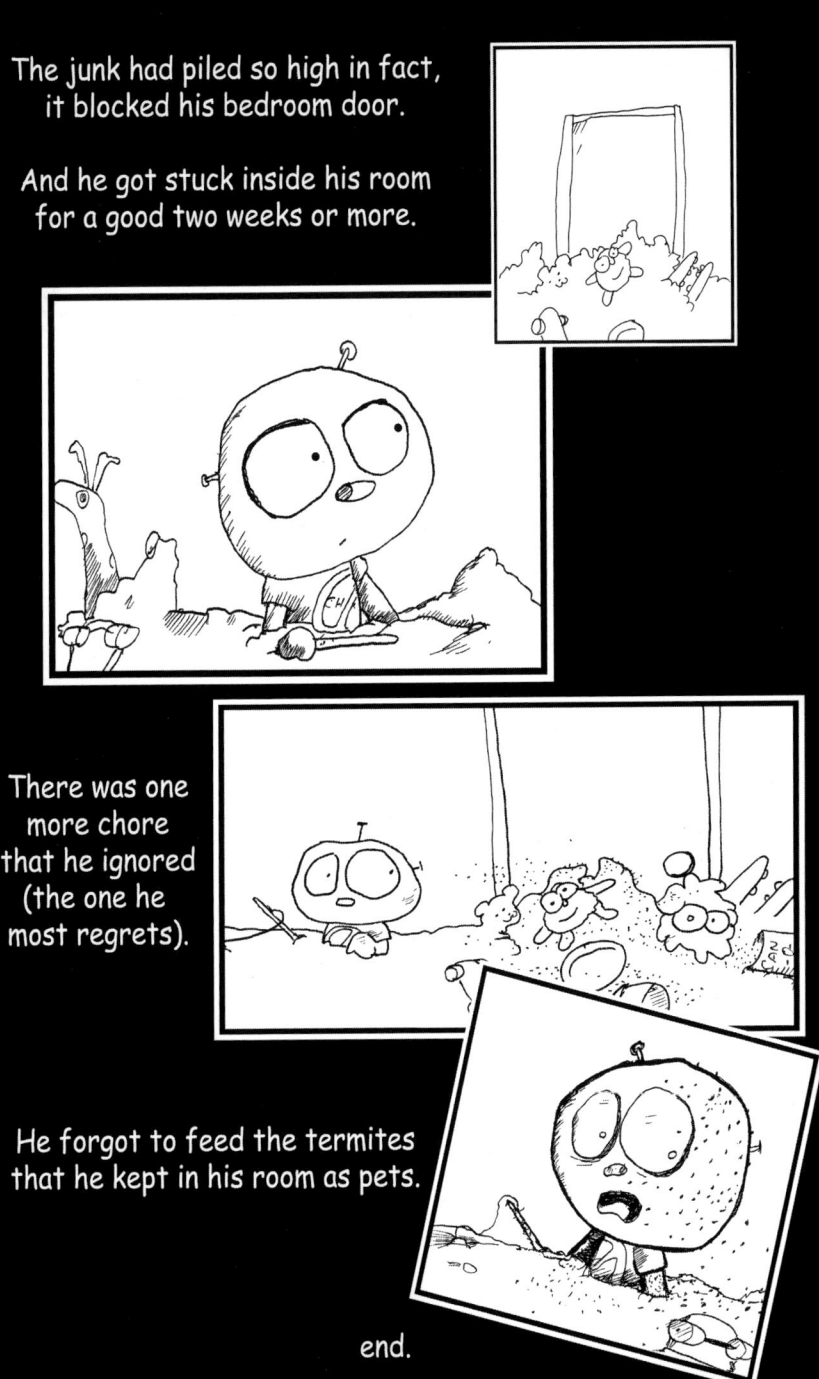

THE OLD WOMAN IN THE SHOE
(REVISITED)

THERE WAS AN OLD WOMAN WHO

LIVED IN A SHOE

SHE HAD SO MANY KIDS

SHE MURDERED A FEW

SHE STARTED WITH TIM

WHO SHE STABBED BY THE LAKE

AND THEN SHE KILLED MIKE

WITH AN OLD RUSTY RAKE

SHE PUT KIM IN THE OVEN

LARRY ON THE STOVE

THEN SHE HIT BOB

WITH THE CAR THAT SHE DROVE

MARLENE AND CHRISTINE

SHE HUNG FROM AN OLD TREE

SHE TIED MATT TO A BRICK

AND THREW HIM IN THE SEA

DISSOLVED LITTLE GARY,

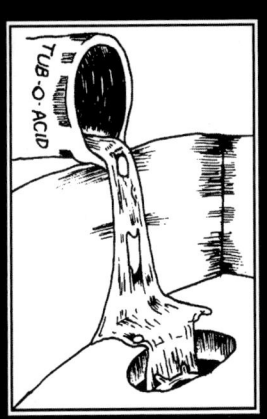

POURED HIM DOWN THE DRAIN

KILLED DANA WITH SCREW WORMS

THAT ATE THROUGH HER BRAIN

SHE PUSHED JEN OFF A CLIFF

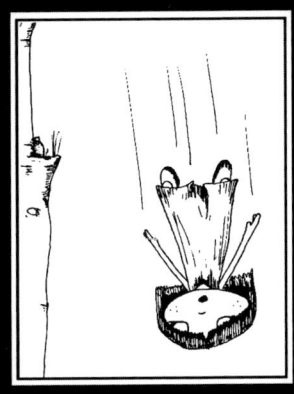

AND SHE DIED VERY FLAT

PLAYED THE WORLD SERIES

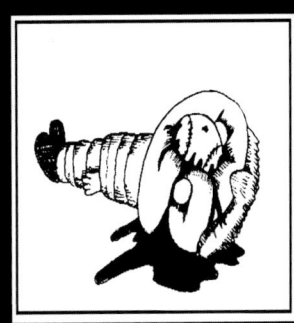

USING RICH AS HER BAT

USING HER VACUUM

SHE SUCKED OUT JOHN'S BREATH

TIED MICHELLE TO A TRUCK

AND DRAGGED HER TO DEATH

MADE HEATHER WEAR RED

TO A BULLFIGHT IN SPAIN

PUSHED KEVIN IN FRONT OF

AN ONCOMING TRAIN

**SCARED VICKY
SO BADLY**

**SHE DIED
OF A STROKE**

**SHE BURNED PAUL
TO DEATH**

**AND KILLED BETH
WITH THE SMOKE**

**SHE PUT
POISONOUS SNAKES**

**INTO CAMI'S
PANTS**

**DIPPED CHERYL
IN HONEY**

**AND FED
HER TO ANTS**

SHE POISONED POOR BRIAN

AND HE DIED VERY SICK

SHE CRUSHED TRISH TO DEATH

WITH A VERY LARGE STICK

WITH AN OLD KNIFE

SHE CUT THE HEAD OFF OF JOE

STABBED APRIL WITH TOOTHPICKS

AND WATCHED HER DIE SLOW

SHE FED LITTLE TRACY  **TO A LION SHE KEPT**	**OVERDOSED DAVE WITH DRUGS** 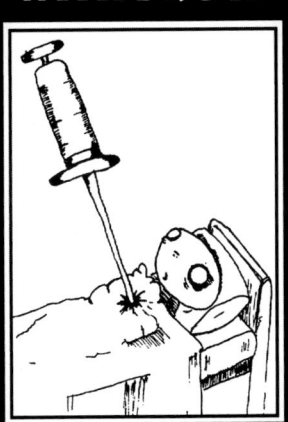 **AT NIGHT WHILE HE SLEPT**
LEFT JONELLE IN THE DESERT  **TO STARVE IN THE SUN**	**THEN SHE SHOT GARRET**  **IN THE HEAD WITH HER GUN**

AS FOR THOMAS AND LISA

SHE MADE THEM DIG THE GRAVES

AND WHEN THEY WERE DONE

SHE SOLD THEM AS SLAVES

WHEN THE KIDS WERE ALL GONE

THE OLD WOMAN WENT HOME

COLLAPSED ON THE FLOOR

AND DIED ALL ALONE

THE SPIDER IN THE BATHROOM

I got up for school this morning
and put on my favorite dress,
went to the bathroom mirror to
make sure I looked my best.
I looked past my reflection,
and in the tub I saw...
The biggest, hairiest, meanest,
looking spider of them all.

So I ran from the bathroom
and started yelling for my dad.

He hadn't had his coffee yet,
so his mood was pretty bad

"what's your problem Elizabeth?"
He yelled back with a growl.

"A goblin? A troll? The Boogey man?
What could it be now?"

I said "It's a big, hairy, spider, dad as big as a horse.
This time I swear I'm not lying dad." he didn't believe
me of course.

He told me to ignore it and that it couldn't be that bad.
I said I could not go in there and he got really mad.

"All right, all right, I'll go in there." He hollered
with a sneer.
"But if you're lying to me again, I'll ground you for
a year."

He abruptly left the table and he stomped across
the floor.
Stomped over to the bathroom and opened up the door.

His bottom jaw dropped open, and his face turned ghostly white.
"**OH MY GOD!**" He shouted, then he whispered "Beth you're right."

The spider was upon him. I guess the shouting made it mad.
Because in less than thirty seconds the spider ate my dad.

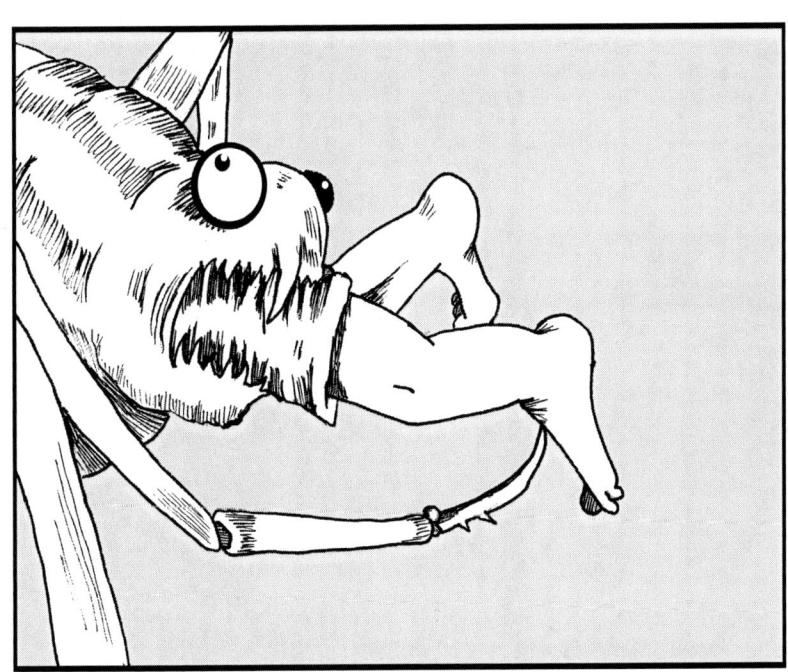

The End.

Mikey

There's a boy down the street I think Mike is his name.
The weird thing about him, is that he really likes pain.

Sometimes you can see him sitting out in the street.
Just rubbing his face in the tar and concrete.

And you'd better be careful when you drive by his house.
He'll run into your car just to knock himself out.

He's got lip rings and earrings, pierced nipples and nose.
He runs around barefoot so he can stub all his toes.

He takes his dad's hammer and smashes his thumbs,
and then he nails toothpicks right into his gums.

There's no time for healing, he just hurts himself more.
Infections are blessings when you like being sore.

Most neighbors enjoy it, they sit back and stare.
And talk of last Christmas when he burned off his hair.

but there's also some neighbors who want him to stop.
And whenever they see him they call for the cops.

Why it would annoy them I really don't know.
I think they should sit back and enjoy the show.

'Cause it's not like he hurts anyone else.
And he gets so much joy out of hurting himself.

When he's done he goes home and puts salt on his wounds.
I hope he'll come back to play again soon.

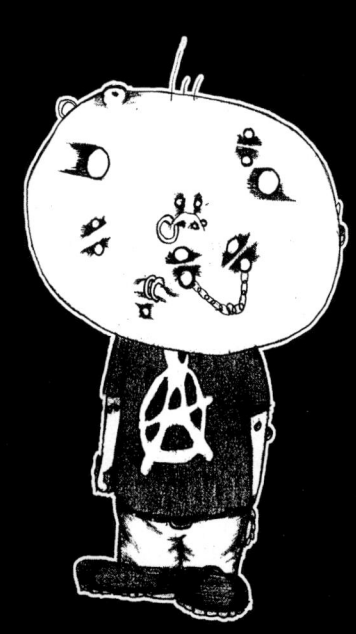

SANTA CLAUS VS. THE C.P.S.C.
(CONSUMER PRODUCT SAFETY COMMISSION)

Twas the night before Christmas and to his dismay,
The C.P.S.C. had seized Santa's sleigh.

"We sent you eight warnings and you didn't comply".
"I never saw them" the jolly man lied.

"These toys are unsafe and they must be destroyed".
"all toys are unsafe?" asked Santa , annoyed.

"Yes" said the king of the C.P.S.C.
"Every toy here can be used lethally".

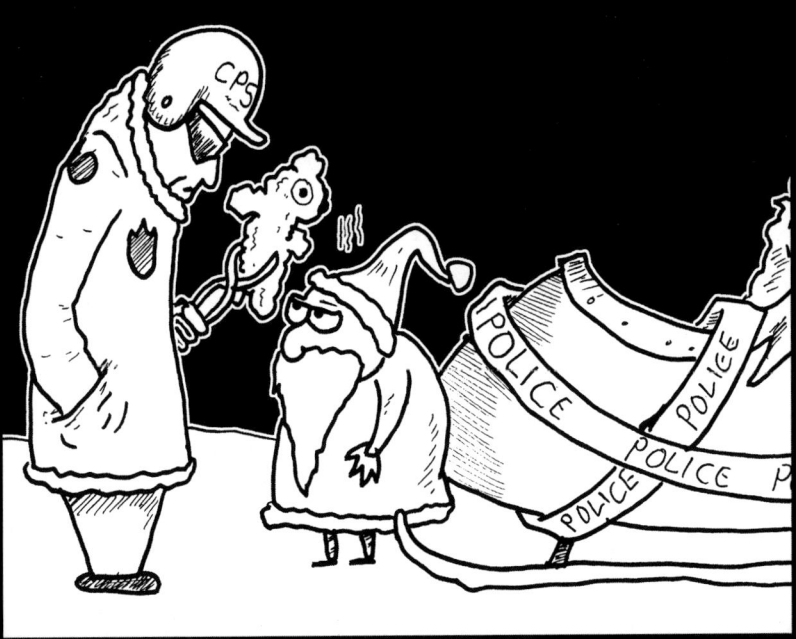

Santa took off his glove, started rubbing his eyes,
And clearly heartbroken he said with a sigh-

"I got rid of weebles, lawn darts and Clackers"
"Easy bake ovens, lead tainted lip smackers"

"I stopped making Lincoln logs because
you told me kids choked"
"Then you took my toy guns, saying
"guns are no joke"

"you can't just come in here and take all my toys"
"What will I give to all the girls and the boys?"

"That's not my problem" the leader replied.
"I don't make the rules, I just abide"

Then he signaled his goons
and they took Santa's toys.
In just a few minutes
the toys were destroyed.

The toy police left as Santa looked on,
Patiently waiting until they were gone.

Then he summoned his elves
and rushed to his home,
opened the door he hid 'neath his throne.

He went to the vault on his top secret floor.
Bashed off the lock and opened the door.

It was filled with banned toys
from Christmases past.
He yelled to his elves to load his sled fast.

They loaded the weebles,
the lawn darts and Clackers
The easy bake ovens
and lead tainted lip smackers.

He thanked all his elves and got into his sleigh,
"the kids will have toys on this Christmas day"

On Christmas morning
the children were stunned.
They got toys that weren't safe,
toys that were fun.

Sure kids got hurt and
a few dumb ones died.
But no one likes dumb kids
and the smart ones survived.

The children grew stronger the country did too.
Because of a fat man who broke all the rules.

Santa went home
and threw back a beer,
Burped, "Merry Christmas to all
and have a Happy New Year".

the end

THE STOPPING OF HAROLD

Johnny McLewski
was not a bad kid.
He just liked to play more than normal kids did.

He hated his schoolwork
and sleep was a bore.
He was always outside ignoring his chores.

Johnny's penchant for pleasure
angered his pop
who tried everything to make his boy stop.

He'd ground him and spank him
and send him to bed.
Instead of his dinner he'd feed him just bread.

He tried being friendly,
he tried being stern,
but try as he might the boy wouldn't learn.

Harold McLewski had done all that he could,
but Johnny, his son, just couldn't be good.

Then one day an ad in the paper appeared,
"YOUR CHILDREN WON'T LISTEN?
Then just bring them here!"

"I am Jaffar the Great, kid fixer supreme!"
"I turn bad young tykes into parenting dreams."

"World famous in Camden,
just ask my close friends,
for a minimal fee your frustration can end."

"That's it!", exclaimed Harold,
he filled up with glee,
"that'll give John the discipline
he desperately needs."

He made an appointment, put the boy in his car,
and sped off to see the world famous Jaffar.

The house of Jaffar was a tattered old shack.
Vines covered the walls
and the windows were black.

Harold was nervous, a little unsure,
as he walked to the shed to knock on the door.

Before he could knock
the door opened wide.
He noticed the shack
was much bigger inside.

"You must be Harold,
and this must be your son,
the one you call Johnny
who only likes fun."

Whispered a voice
from out of the air,
"He is", replied Harold,
a little bit scared.

He was looking at Johnny
and rubbing his brow,
"Your child is broken?
Please tell me how."

"He's reckless", said Harold,
"and always at play",
"He keeps putting his chores off
day after day."

"Your boy just sounds normal",
the blue man replied,
"but since you are paying,
I'll be on your side."

He grabbed hold of Johnny
and he said a few words.
They were in a strange language
that Harold never heard

"I'm Jaffar the Great
and I've just fixed your boy."
"I'm sure", muttered Harold
who was getting annoyed.

"Tomorrow he'll listen; in the morning you'll see,
now please pay Jaffar the agreed upon fee."

Harold reluctantly paid the strange skinny man.
He couldn't believe he fell for this scam.

When Johnny awoke to the mid-morning sun,
he snuck past his dad to go have some fun.

He went out to play with the neighborhood kids,
he noticed a sign that said "STOP" and he did.

He stood without moving
while the other kids played.
He stood there for hours,
he stood there all day.

When the sun had gone down
and the street lights came on,
he stayed standing still,
despite calls from his mom.

She called him and called him
then yelled for his dad,
"Harold!", she yelled,
"Your son's being bad!"

His father was angry,
as you might have guessed.
He had just gotten home
and was trying to rest.

He stomped out the door
with a growl and a moan
to search for his boy
and to bring him back home.

"Johnny!" he yelled,
(because that was his name),
"You'd better come home,
son! This isn't a game!"

That's when he saw him
standing under the sign,
down at the corner
of Main Street and Pine.

He called him again
but his son did not move,
which as you can guess,
didn't brighten his mood.

He pushed him and pulled him,
he gave him a nudge,
but try as he might, the boy would not budge.

"I'm calling Jaffar! This is not what I meant."
said Harold, upset, over the money he'd spent.

When he dialed the number, no one was there.
No ringing, no tone, just empty dead air.

He called 411 and for the number insisted,
they told him the number had never exhisted.

A few weeks had passed
and the boy was still there.
A couple of birds made their nest in his hair.

The police tried to move him
but it could not be done,
so he stood there all summer
in the heat of the sun.

And because of the taunting
that grew every day,
his parents went mad and were taken away.

When summer had ended
to welcome the fall,
he was still at the stop sign, not moving at all.

Since a good way to move him
just could not be found,
the lawyers proclaimed he belonged to the town.

And at the weekly town meeting,
Mayor McBlight,
had Johnny declared a new tourist site.

They built him a shelter with heating and air,
cleaned up his clothes
and took the birds from his hair.

Soon busloads of tourists would start coming by
and the Mayor made sure
they had keepsakes to buy.

They sold T-shirts with captions,
(in Braille for the blind),
that said, "I love the boy
who stands still by the sign."

At first the town loved it,
a quaint passing fad,
but when folks started camping
it got really bad.

They camped all around him
and clogged up the streets.
They threw presents and flowers
and coins at his feet.

They grew into a cult
and without wasting time,
they became "The Church
of the Boy by the Sign".

The cultists were praying
and kissing his shoes.
They called him a God
and it got on the news.

When the news told the world,
even more came to see
the mysterious boy
who stood as still as could be.

By the time winter came
the whole town was annoyed,
the streets grew so crowded
Marines were deployed.

The garbage had piled up ten miles high.
It got to the point you could not see the sky.

Houses were trampled and kicked to the ground.
Poor Mayor McBlight was chased out of town.

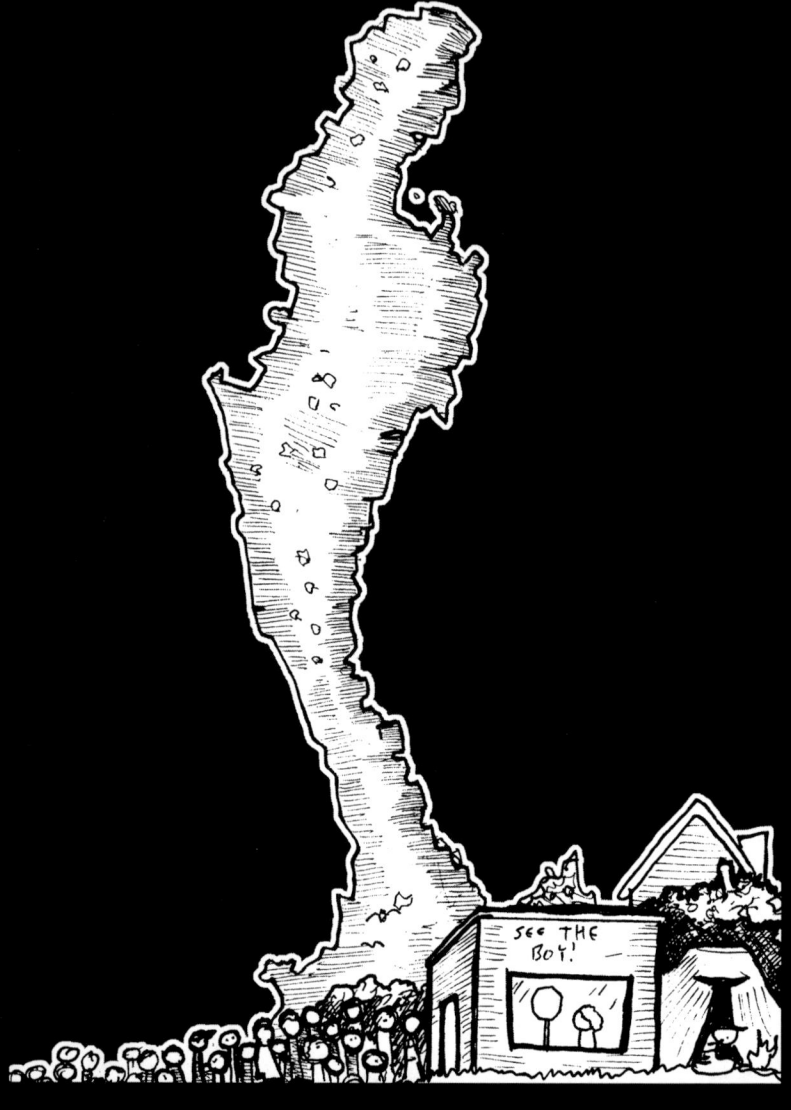

Then something odd happened
no one could foretell.

A gust of wind blew
and that old stop sign fell.

When the sign hit the ground
we all were surprised
to see the boy yawning
and rubbing his eyes.

While the boy was still yawning,
a strange man appeared;
a skinny blue man
with a lengthy black beard.

He looked out at the people
and was clearly annoyed.
He picked up the presents,
the coins and the boy.

"You're wasting your children",
he said with a sneer.
Then the boy
and the coins
and the man
disappeared.

fin.

NEIGHBORS

When I was just a little boy, a couple days past four,
the strangest folks I'd ever seen moved in the house next door.

Now when I say "folks" don't get me wrong they weren't like you or me.
As a matter of fact they were crocodiles and just as big as they could be.

The mommy croc' was ten feet tall,
the daddy was eleven.

The youngest son was five foot three,
the oldest one was seven.

As they moved in, my parents watched,
they just stood and stared.

My dad said "I don't like this",
my mom said "Hank I'm scared".

The next few weeks at my house were very, very weird.
Mom wouldn't leave the window and dad drank lots of beer.

"How could a crocodile buy a house?" Asked dad, "I't doesn't make much sense."

"I don't know dear." Mom replied, sounding kind of tense.

Then one day the doorbell rang. And although no one was there,

we found a message taped to the door, the headline read "WE CARE".

"What is that?" I asked my dad. He said it was a note.

"It's from those crazy crocs' next door, I'll read you what they wrote."

"It says 'Dear beloved neighbors, we've just moved into town.
So we're sending out this letter to invite all of you down

to our house next Friday night, we'll eat and chat a while.
Hope to see you there new friend. Signed Mr. Crocodile".

"I don't trust 'em Hank," said my mom, "it just does not seem right".

"I agree with you." dad said, "we'll stay home this Friday night".

Friday came and as usual my mom watched through the glass.

As on their way to the Crocodile's house all the neighbors passed.

I saw old Mr. Johnson and a lot of kids from school.
I kind of wished my mom would've let me go to dinner too.

They must have been great dinner hosts, well that's what I believe.
Because we saw the neighbors go inside but we never saw them leave.

end

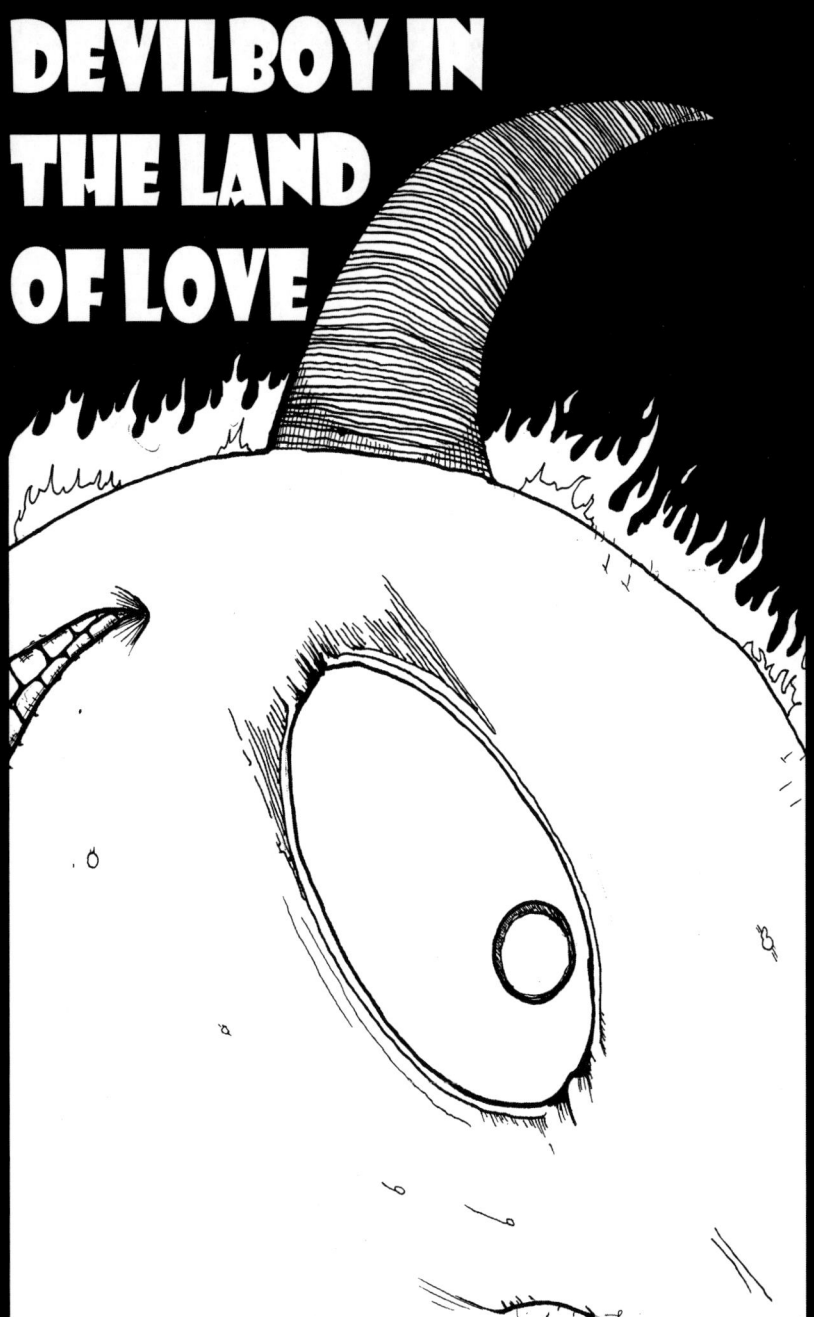

This story takes place in a place down below.
A dark scary place where the bad people go.

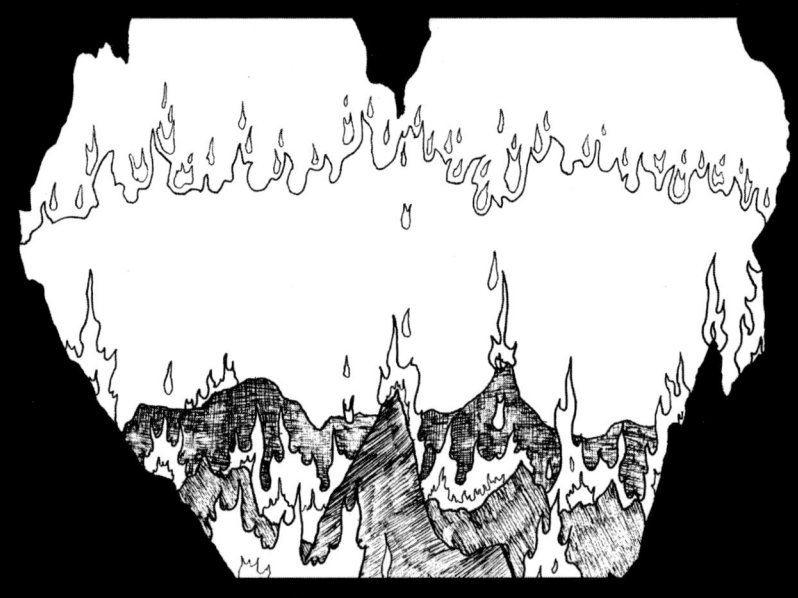

Not that long ago in a place we call Hell.
Among the ashes, the heat and the smell,

**Lived a very young boy,
aged only eight months past three.
Only he was not a normal kid
like you or me.**

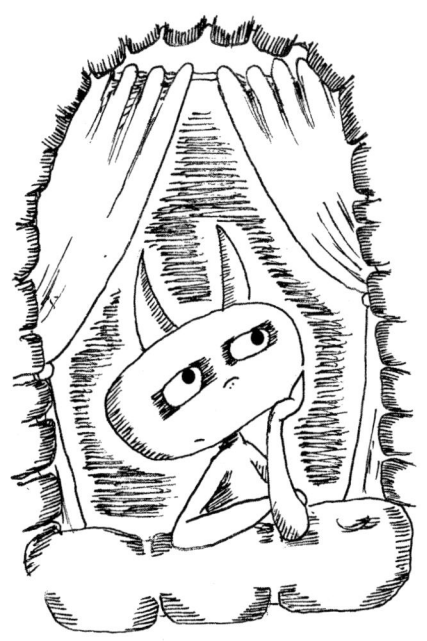

**His skin was dark red
and he had a horn over each eye.
Because his father was Satan,
the Dark Lord of Lies.**

**He would sit in his room, day in and day out.
He would stare out the window, just sit
there and pout**

He was supposed to be evil,
but he just didn't care.
He longed to see sunshine
and breathe some fresh air.

He heard all the stories
of the land up above.
Stories of laughter
and something called love.

So he just sat in his room
in his creaky old chair,
and he thought about how nice
his life would be up there

Away from these smells,
the smoke and the screams.
And away from his dad
because he was so darn mean.

He just sat in his room,
he sat there and stared.
feeling distracted, bored and
despaired.

As he sat there thinking
his father burst in.
Home from a long day
of making folks sin.

He looked at his son
and started yelling and screaming.
"How could you sit here all day,
just daydreaming?"

"When there are killers to torment
and lawyers to gore,
How could you sit here
ignoring your chores?"

"You get me so mad son,
because you don't understand,
That when I've passed on
you'll inherit this land."

"But I don't want your hell."
Devilboy had replied
As tears welled up
in his cold, dark, black eyes.

"It's all good for you dad,
you're used to this hell,
with all of the torture,
the heat and the smell."

"I long for the world
with it's lakes and it's skies.
I don't want to live here
as the next King of Lies."

His father just sat there
and he looked really pissed.
Then finally he yelled,
raising his fist.

"If you feel that you must
see the real world that bad"
"Then go there, and stay!
I'm no longer your dad."

So he packed up his things
and left the room where he stayed.
A little excited
and a little afraid.

He hoped that the world
was all that he'd heard,
he couldn't wait to meet people,
see puppies and birds.

As he walked out of Hell
through all of the gates,

He thought about life
without anger and hate.

He was walking and thinking
about people and love.
When he came to the ladder
that led up above.

He paused for a moment
and thought of his dad.
"He was mean but I'll miss him,"
and the thought made him sad.

He started to climb,
and as he exited Hell,
Something was different
in the air that he smelled.

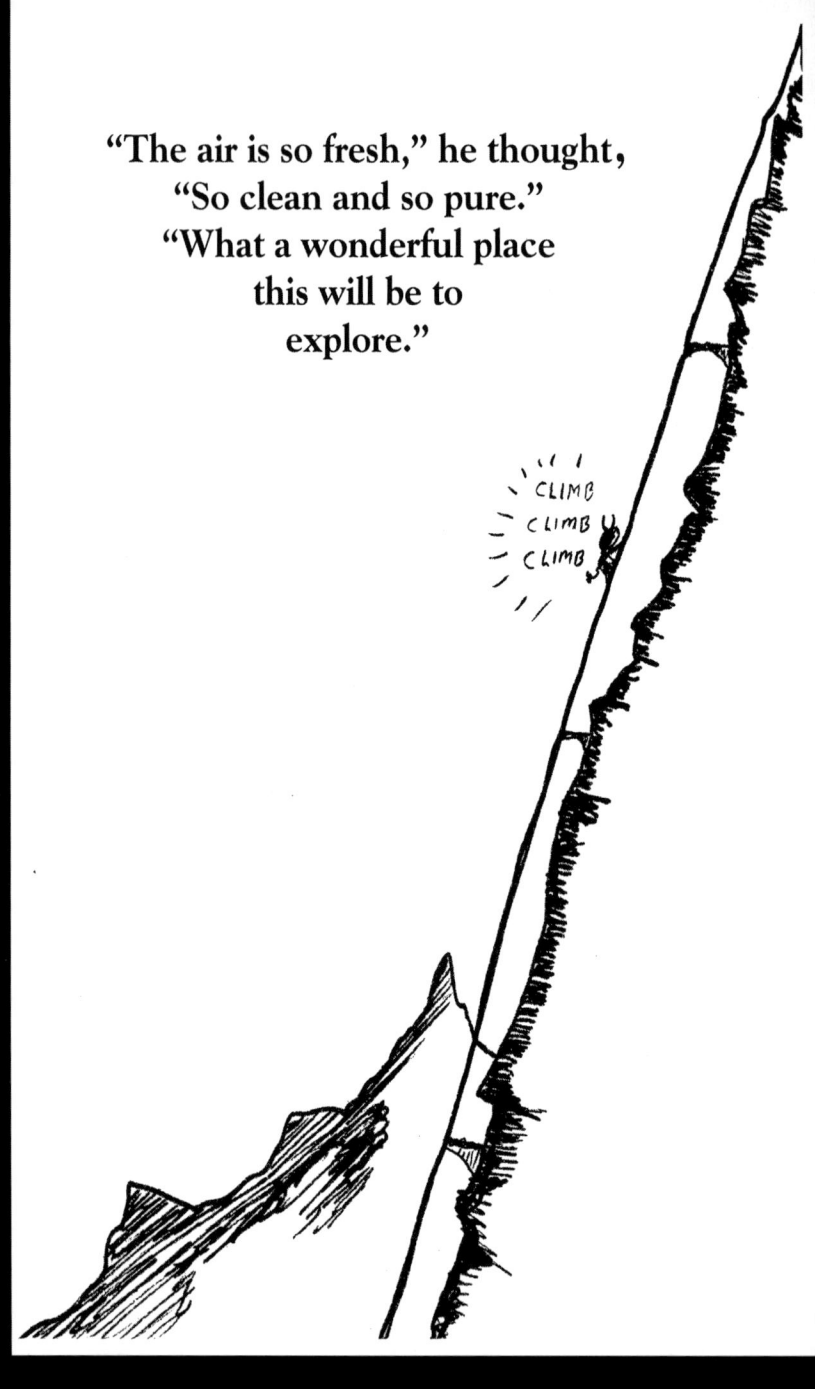

And right up above him, in fact,
just over his head.
There was a door with an exit sign
that glowed crimson red.

He climbed up to the door,
and with a push and a shove . . .
He was finally there.
He was finally above.

Now he felt something
his dad would never abide.
For the first time in his life
he was happy inside.

Then he heard something.
Was it true? Could it be?
He ran through the bushes
to get closer and see.

YES! There were people
and they were talking of love.
They talked of forgiveness
and a God from above.

They sang and they listened
to a man dressed in black.
He said their sins were forgiven
and to never look back.

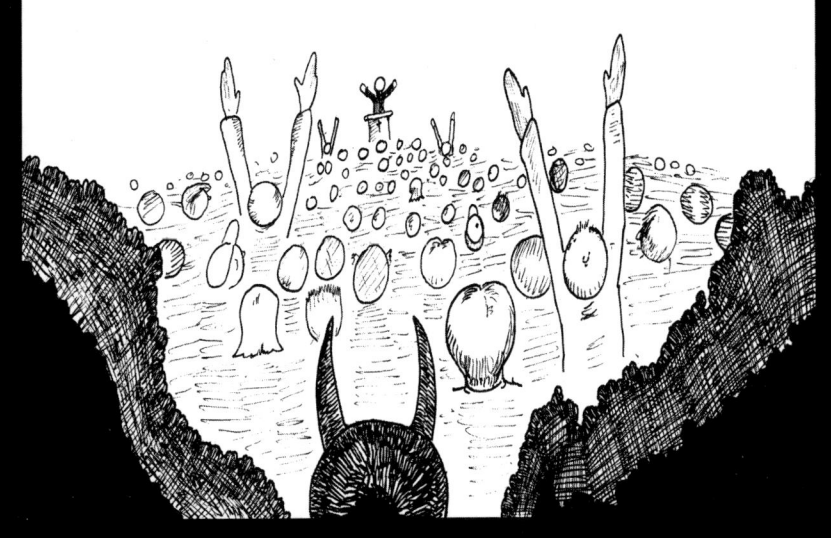

"Their sins are forgiven?" He thought,
"Now that's for me!"
"It's time to go meet
all these people I see."

So to them he walked
with his smile spread wide.
That's when they stopped talking
and the all moved aside.

"Oh my God, it's the devil!"
The man in black yelled.
"We have to kill him right now,
or he'll take us to Hell!"

The church folk attacked him,
with Bibles in hand.

They beat him and kicked him
and shoved his face in the sand

They dragged him and tied him
to a post in the ground.

"BURN HIM!" they chanted,
as they threw some wood down.

He stared at them sadly,
too frightened to speak.

And the beatings he'd gotten
had made him quite weak.

He thought "so much for laughter
and stories of love."

"There's nothing but hate
in this land up above."

They lit him on fire.
He burned as they cheered.

He died scared and lonely
without shedding a tear.

They were beaming with pride
as the flames burned his skin.

'Cause they could brag to their friends
how they saved us from sin.

end

Thank you

Thanks for reading (and buying) this book. If you are one of the people who bought any of the previous Odd Tales books, you will notice that I left most of the original illustrations. I did that for two reasons, 1. Even though I might hate the original artwork, I know from your letters some of you got a kick out of it. And 2, I'm really lazy.

I also didn't put the books in chronological order because I wanted to end the book with the Devilboy story.

Here is a list of when the books came out and what was in them. Any story that isn't mentioned is either new to this book or from the TPB collection that came out in 2001.

Devilboy in the Land of Love 1996
Featured Zombie Girl, Melissa, Spider in the Bathroom, Death (comic), Mikey & Sisters.

The Boy who ate the World 1997
Featured Neighbors, Edge of the World, Safety, Forbidden Love, The Wooden Boy and Braggart (comic)

The Old Woman in the Shoe 1999
Just the title poem showing all my friends getting murdered. No extra poems, it's my least favorite of all the books.

The Snow Prince 2001
The only non-rhyming Odd tale, it featured A book for Nicole.

The Stopping of Harold 2006
Featured just the title poem.

Santa vs. the C.P.S.C. (mini book) 2010
A mini comic that we gave out to guests of our annual Happy Drunk Xmas Party that we have every year at the Asbury Lanes in Asbury Park, NJ.

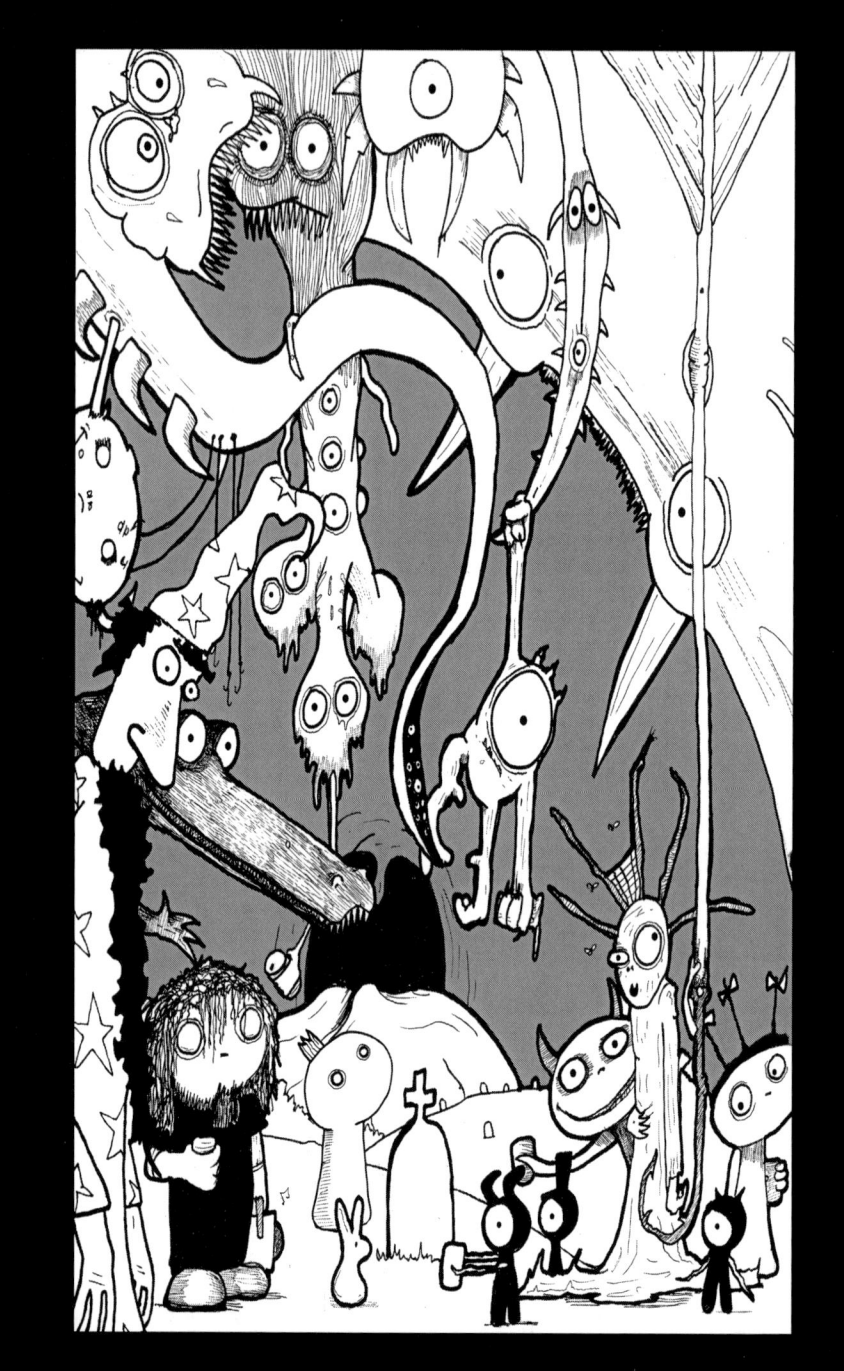